A PERFECT DESIGN

J. ROD

A perfect design
J. Rod

First edition July 2020
First published Mexico City, July 2020

"I could not dedicate this work to anyone other than the one who has always accompanied me in my life, in any project, on any green or winding road, I dedicate this novel to God because he has given me inspiration in each of the wonders of the nature."

INDEX

A PERFECT DESIGN

J. ROD

Chapter 1. That ritual called routine

Year 2023

Every evening, when sunset is lilac, I walk the same path again. I have traveled it for 1,826 days. Just today I am five years of searching in the horizon for the signal that brings me back to life.

For many impatient, 1,826 days is too long. It was like the blink of an eye. Many would also think that hope decreases every day. And that would be logical, but I come to each sunset, equal or more motivated than the day before. Maybe this day is the right one.

Although I don't enjoy the tasteless aroma given off by any object touched by sea salt, feeling the breeze on my face lightens any discomfort. I have added some amenities to enjoy the wait a little. I selected special music for the road from St. Martin ridge to the lighthouse. It was difficult to choose between so many songs that evoke her memory, especially since in addition to the classic ones of some anniversary or birthday; they were heard in 10 years together. There were even some of salsa, reggaeton, hard rock or classical, genres that were not to my liking, and yet, even in those categories there was the odd song that reminded me of her smile or some anecdote with her.

I also bought comfortable tennis shoes to cover long distances, without shoelaces, which reduced the time to get from my house, a few blocks above the beach.

At first I came very formal, in a suit and tie, despite the intense heat of my land and because at that moment my life was pouring out. The occasion warranted it.

However, I thought that it is something material because where I will go with her I will not need any of this. I'd rather pay attention to always carry my favorite moisturizers, even enjoying a hot chocolate or a double espresso or toasting with a glass of Carmenere wine. I know it sounds crazy, but I had no other fun, so I took advantage of those moments to feel good. Dark grapes and Dutch cheese completed the menu on days when I was more motivated.

I also got a thick and tough violet raincoat for those days that abound in winter, with strong winds from the north and rains that cool the weather, even when it is always warm. Here people freeze at 18 degrees Celsius.

When it rains slowly you can feel a moment of peace and harmony, as if the water cleanses the soul and each drop purifies the beach. The breeze brings with it a unique aroma. I carry black coffee in a thermos so that its smell and taste stimulate my senses on that long walk and blow my mind. That's when I find answers; with the gray horizon in the background.

Today was a very productive day, despite having spilled my coffee when tripping over a marble stone, from a piece of cracked boardwalk, before entering the arena. I smiled as if I had seen the scene in the distance of a stumbling idiot. My motivation increased every year, and I thought positively about how to start this cycle again.

A homeless old man approached me at the end of my routine. I had spent years observing him, there, facing the sea, prostrate in a corner of the old coastal boardwalk. Its stench was unmatched, aged by sea salt.

When I had to pass near him, I crossed the sidewalk. I did not remember if he was there before starting my routine of the last five years or a little later. I only know that it was suddenly customary for me to see him.

That afternoon I approached him, because the wooden carriage where they sold the elixir that is extracted from coconuts, and that was my breakfast, was almost on one side of his territory, of his room. The coconut seller was not located at the same distance as always because when winds from the North are predicted they are located more to the East so as not to be affected.

That delicious aged water passed through my pupils and my throat. It was invigorating to drink after a long walk. I took the last sip, shuddering with that bittersweet taste, and then returned home.

-The day is near,- the old man told me with a hoarse and disheveled voice that puzzled me for an instant. Then I sensed that every word in that daily ritual would interpret or encase it in the meaning of my daily visits to the sea. I did not care and continued on my way home.

- I repeat that your day is near,- he insisted, taking me by the arm. In his eyes I saw something different from what was expected of him: a deep tranquility. So I was not bothered by his abruptness.

- Tell me, sir, what are you saying? - I answered kindly.

-You know what I'm talking about, Juan Martín.

When I heard my name, the presence of the old man filled me with confidence. But how did this stranger know my name? I'm not even half known in the city.

- Yes, I know you - he said to me in a slow voice -, and I know what you are looking for on the horizon. It seems impossible to believe that crazy theory, but you are close to finding it. Sometimes it happens every 150 years. No one lives that time, nor does have the patience to wait for it. So there is no witness to it. However, you are close to finding that color that is missing on the horizon.

The mysterious old man walked away and disappeared among the palm trees. I was speechless by his revelations. How could he know what I was looking for? Perhaps he was also delusional believing that complex theory.

I don't know, but his words, his conviction, his way of holding on just like me, made me have more hope. My chest swelled with immense energy each time I breathed in the deliciously cool winter breeze.

Only a dreamer could believe the crazy words of a homeless person, however, hearing those words caused a stream of fresh air to inflate my body to burst with so much emotion.

In my ears resounded the almost made manifest voice of the old man: "The day is near! The day is near! The day is near!" I even felt her arms merge with the breeze. My skin tingled. It was the perfect combination of shades in the sky: brown, reddish, violet, red, light blue, strong, faint yellow, almost imperceptible, greyish, until it was lost in the black night, as a sign that invited me not to decline in my daily crusade.

I had seen all the sunsets surrounding the beach. However, in recent years I only expected that divine sign.

This could be the most romantic story. Sometimes it is frustrating waiting or not understanding the reason of things. It was a hard story to discover universal secrets that would border on insanity and all for not accepting the daily truth and holding on to see her at any cost.

Sometimes I still doubt even with so much evidence, but I have faith because everything I discovered reading Hawking changed my outlook on life. And I clung to each of those concepts, some I couldn't even understand, but I did it and asked so many questions, the conclusion of which led me to this daily ritual for her.

As I have written, it is not a romantic journey; it is one of visualizing so many possibilities in the universe that it can be too complex and difficult to understand. Bringing together so many concepts of our planet and soul is something that may sound crazy. I did and decided to fervently believe in that crazy theory.

Although the journey is not romantic, if I manage to find that color at the end of the horizon I will be successful and it will not be the most romantic story in the world, but it is the most moving end and therefore I toast each night under the stars.

Chapter 2. My theory

Year 2018

I did not try to plagiarize the title of the work of the genius of cosmological science, Stephen Hawking, but his theory was partial to me, even though he was one of the most intelligent men in the world.

It posed a whole linked to matter and the universe as the ideal place to be the home of human beings. As if the most important thing in that universe was the stars, the black holes, gravity and not the species. It would also be a partial vision to think only of humans and leave aside the complex understanding of the universe. I don't know how I started to philosophize on these issues that I didn't even understand. It was like an instinct that forced me to do it.

I walked along the boardwalk of the city observing the intense yellow of the early spring sun and listening to the noise of the great waves of the sea. It was my daily route to exercise and relax from any stress. On that boulevard I had lived the biggest dreams of my life. So the landscape calmed me down and filled me with nostalgia for the reunion with my past. From when I was a child walking with my father in the morning, as a teenager celebrating the victories of the Mexican Soccer Team, sometimes as a young man waiting for the sunrise of each first day of the year and as an adult enjoying the sunset together.

Some Sunday mornings, I ran several kilometers along the beach, surrounding the sea, from the ridge to the lighthouse. That feeling of relief in the body, after intense exercise caused me great joy. And the elixir to extend that feeling of hubbub was a double espresso from an Italian coffee shop located just at the beginning of the journey.

Sitting, with my gaze lost in the sea, I felt that magnetic need to turn to look anywhere, as when someone is staring at you. I thought immediately of some old friendship, a love from the past, but I was wrong.

On a shelf, where they placed books and magazines to leaf through, they had put up for sale some works by popular authors of various genres. A cover captivated me. Observing the name of one of the brightest minds in the world, but especially the title of the text, prompted me to enter the cafeteria and enjoy that pleasant aroma of paper from books, which is as stimulating as the smell of coffee or chocolate. I took it and immediately went to the cashier to pay for it. I didn't even notice the price. I was very excited to read the work of a brilliant mind that we would no longer see in the world. He had recently died. Stephen Hawking's "The theory of everything" felt like velvet in my hands.

I returned to sit at the table outside the cafeteria and began reading the prologue to a work that transformed my life and perhaps that of the planet.

The play was an attempt to unify the forces of nature into a single theory, that of the Whole, but it was not the prologue that puzzled me, but Stephen's epitaph was the formula for entropy of black holes.

$$S_{BH} = 1/4 \ (c^2 \ k) \ / \ (4h \ G) \ A$$

Who would put a formula on his grave? Instead of a familiar phrase, a verse, or a dedication.

I was shocked by the argument and so I set out to develop a hypothesis of fact. I had to argue that this formula was more than an engraving in a pantheon, but a hidden message from someone with an overflowing IQ and an eccentric way of thinking. I felt that there was something more to that combination of letters and numbers. I raised it from the beginning of my reading. It could be a key, an orientation, a location, for someone who believed space-time had several dimensions. Perhaps it was a message for the future.

The book was a compilation of seven of his lectures. That day I read the first two that contained concepts already known since my student days.

In the first lecture, Hawking led me by the hand for unknown concepts, but always basing his theories to determine that the universe was expanding. It was not static, nor was it invariable.

I read a phrase that gave me confidence, from my Catholic faith, to continue reading: "*an expanding universe does not exclude the figure of a Creator, but it limits when he could have done his work.*" I think that a scientific work excluding our Creator is empty and does not motivate me to read it.

I read the first lecture in 30 minutes. The sun's rays brought out the best nuances from the sky above the sea, yet I couldn't stop thinking about her. In each book I looked for an answer. Where would she be right now?

Lecture two posed the question: *"Will the universe stop expanding and begin to contract or will it expand forever?"* And he urged to argue a beginning of our universe, *"however, the mathematical theorem does not admit discussion, so now it is generally accepted that the universe should have a beginning"*.

The following textual quote motivated me to accelerate my reading: *"what we can be really sure of is that, even if the universe is going to collapse again, it will not do so for at least another 10 billion years, since it has already been expanding for at least that time. This should not worry us too much, since, by then, unless we have colonies beyond the solar system, humanity will have disappeared long ago, extinct with the death of our Sun"*.

Since I was a child I have fervently believed in the possibility that we are not the only beings in the universe. I know that to a certain extent it is a limited paradigm to think of the human being as the only thinking being in so many light years. But not only did I think about life in other places in space, but as I read lecture three I was developing a slight hope of seeing her one day. That thought sounded crazy, but I couldn't stop trying whatever it was to have her with me again.

Every page read was an answer for me. Each word was thought in the moment of uncertainty and pain that I was experiencing after two years of losing her. I ordered a milk coffee and a lemon pie to continue enjoying the reading of that Hawking manifesto until I finally got to know what the concept so mysterious in science and so cited, black holes, *"name coined by John Wheeler and whose definition was a star that was sufficiently massive and compact would have a gravitational field so intense that light could not escape. That's what they are: black voids in space."* The definition was not very clear to me, especially since I did not master these topics; however, as I continued reading I found some magic in that concept. I drank a sip of coffee almost for every page read, for the anxiety of discovering new things.

"A star forms when a large amount of gas, primarily hydrogen, begins to collapse on itself due to its gravitational pull," the book said.

I took a big sip. A little sweat dripped from my forehead, so I took off my cap bearing the logo of my university, and read in slow motion:

"In this way, there is a set of events, a region of space time, from which it is not possible to escape to reach a distant observer. This region is what we call a black hole. If any version of the censorship hypothesis were valid, the consequences would be enormous because near naked singularities, it may be possible to travel to the past, which would mean that no life would be safe forever. This would offer great possibilities for time travel in space. "

My gaze remained lost on the sunny horizon, imagining a future with her, our life together. My chest was about to explode from the arousal of my deepest thoughts, and I could almost feel her lips when everything was gone.

-Excuse me; can I serve you something else? - The waitress of the place said to me over and over again. I was baffled, barely able to coordinate.

- No, miss, thank you very much- I replied, stammering a bit, while looking at the hands on my watch that marked a quarter before noon. I had to return home to continue with some pending work, however, the moment was magical for imagining her and feeling her aroma in the coffee.

-Only the bill, miss, please. - I took the last few sips of my milk coffee and started walking towards my house.

There was a great noise in the city, much to be Sunday. I noticed the church more crowded than usual. Outside, the whispering of the parishioners was heard more than the priest's sermon, despite his powerful microphone.

I kept going, with my faith in God a bit undermined, however, I felt stupid trying to carry on a fight against the one who had given me her, although later he took her from me, an immense happiness of many years with her, and that was something of indescribable value.

For this I did not stop thanking God and cross myself when I passed through the church. I was walking fast so as not to run into someone I knew and listen to the same stories, although due to the smell of the marquesitas I was tempted to stop.

Back home, I remembered the most important moments with her. Although it was a pure, perfect relationship, there were moments marked by an innate sexual attraction, never felt synchrony and that is why those images were the first to come to my memory.

Chapter 3. Extreme fascination

Year 2010

It's perhaps the most striking image my experienced pupils have ever observed. For me, personally, it is also the most plethora of art on the face of the Earth. Her green eyes dotted with light grey like the Caribbean Sea pigmented by sand, showed a mixture of surprise and admiration. She had never done that ritual, where yes, she would swear it was her first time with me, that the first intimate part that touched her lips and licked her tongue was mine.

Sometimes I felt it as a test of her love for me, something that wasn't usual, perhaps very private. My fascination was not only because she did it with me but apart from becoming addicted to having me inside her mouth, she probably got to prefer it more than kissing me which was already an affront because she loved to stick to my lips and tell me *"give me a good kiss."* It was a delight to feel the unmatched smoothness of her lips and at the same time that unique scent in the world of her body and perfume, while the fingertips of my fingers could touch any part of her body without inhibition and my eyes looked at her eyelids squeezing with the intensity of my kisses. The sound of her lips wanting to devour mine sometimes haunted me on sleepless nights and my excitement lasted the whole night, contrasting with that delicate almost imperceptible sound of her lips rubbing my limb from the tip to the deepest part. I don't know if it was her throat that I felt when it came across something, but that feeling was amazing.

I was proud of what I had achieved, although at times I also sick to think like this and make her addicted to sucking my penis all day, however it was a fact, I had made her an expert in that activity, well I do not know if in that activity in general or only had she become a professional in giving me pleasure, and is that there was no greater pleasure in the world than being inside her, but before that there was the ritual of her mouth devouring my most intimate part. I noticed the difference between the first few times when she could barely talk about it and even hurt me with her teeth and instead of feeling pleasure I felt pain, but I shaped her in that art until I achieved a spectacular pleasure of just watching her approach her mouth to me.

That day the ritual was crazy, she made me explode like a teenager earlier than expected and it was that I was not in my plans to do it that way but to date I do not remember a more delicious moment feeling her saliva running every inch of my erect skin, but above all that unmatched smoothness of her tongue paddling every nerve of my limb. And not only that excited my senses, but also listening to her breathing, it was not a hectic breath of tiredness, it was a hectic breath of pleasure, she was enjoying it as much as I was. Barely reached to see her face because her hair covered most of the scene, however I saw her naked body in all its splendor, her skin bristling at the feeling of my fingertips barely slightly rubbing her waist as I smelled the scent of her perfume and her parts intimate combined.

The scene became perfect when the sound of raindrops on a spring night began to touch the window and watched each drop drain imagining her saliva and tongue draining the same way from the tip to the base. It was so vivid that moment that every time I remember it my senses get excited to the fullest, sometimes I even have an ejaculation unintentionally and I must immediately return to my house to change my clothes. That day the climax didn't happen at the usual climax moment, it happened moments later.

It was an afternoon like any of our other chance encounters in that uninhabited big house from which my best friend had lent me the keys and where we saw each other almost daily after leaving both of work, the advantage was his location just two blocks from her Office. Time was always our worst enemy, her parents didn't usually leave her alone, so we came as thirsty to a sea and opened the door so quickly that we sometimes accidentally left the door ajar. We ran up the stairs to the top floor of the house, to the room at the end which was the narrowest, that sky of the house also became my sky where I lived the best moments of my life, sometimes the air conditioning didn't cool the room, we just stayed there for a lot thirty or forty minutes. She adored kissing first of all, it was almost a demand of the ritual, she melted my kisses, she took away her clothes voraciously before the rush of time and kissed her breast, her waist until I reached her lower lips which I kissed and undone with my tongue. You could find every trigger of your groans and your breathing accelerated.

That occasion when I noticed her completely excited and could even observe the bones of her ribs as I performed such deep breaths when my tongue circularly grazed that little lump in the midst of her intimacy, I took her hair and pulled her head towards me while I lay down, she didn't even question it, she was automatically guided with the force of my hands in her hair. What a delight to feel her tongue wrapped in my member! It was the only moment in my life when I forgot everything around, there were no problems or worries, just the pleasure of being with her without inhibitions, my mind at that time was incapable of processing any thought, it was only pleasure that guided me and I freaked out as she moved her head from one side to the other.

Usually she would walk her tongue multiple times until I took her hand and pushed her away from there to whip her against the bed and penetrate her with all my might by adding the strength of the weight of my body on her.

That occasion was different, turning my gaze down and seeing her light green-grey eyes exalted as her lips stretched out with all her might to make me happy. That image changed everything, the most exciting moment of our encounters changed, my mind felt her tongue wet and soft sliding down every part of my skin rubbing every nerve sent a sign that I could not contain myself, I felt like a soldier in front of the wall , feeling as every bullet entered my body until I left lifeless, the bullets from the raindrops hitting my head, the bullets from her eyes intimidating mine, the bullets of uncontainable pleasure in every inch of my skin, the bullets of her hair tangling in me , the bullets in my mind feeling the vibration of the sound of her breathing, the bullets from her crotch grazing the fingertips of my fingers, I could not do too much! I squeezed the pillow strong with my left hand to the side of the bed that she and I were doing that night, with a massive force like letting go of my life completely in that movement and in that spontaneous groan of my voice.

Ecstasy is the most exciting moment of any relationship but there was a moment, when I felt I couldn't contain myself, that unbearable tingle of pleasure that made me automatically pull her hair with my right hand barely with the force of the exhausted of pleasure that was. Barely she could breathe, she had lost her breath, she did not plan to move and I did not want to ejaculate inside her mouth just wanted her tingling to stop to enjoy that feeling, that orgasm in every expulsion so I just gave her hair a tug so that I drop.

And there I was writhing with pleasure when the first fountain sprouted from the tip of my being at an unimaginable speed. My eyes were closed as I passed that first expulsion of semen and I felt an endless orgasm, at that moment I turned to see her, totally surrendered in bed and that image went on to the posterity of my days.

It's indelible she was just tattooed in my eyes, I looked down to see what I was doing as I enjoyed every spasm and had my gaze lost in that boiling volcano, every squirt emanating from the tip of my intimate part, she looked stunned, perplexed, she looks like a little child fascinated by fireworks in a celebration when it has never seen them before, with an inexplicable admiration and emotion, I only saw those beautiful green pupils increase in size in the face of the fascination of seeing me ejaculate, her fixed gaze did not blink surprised by the effect of her tongue. I could even have an instant look at the reflection of that bud through its clear pupils, as if looking at the illuminated moon through the clear glass of a window. So she was shocked to see up and down every outbreak that even robbed her of a slight spontaneous and innocent smile, the boiling lasted longer than usual perhaps because of the effect of observing it, I wish I would never end and dehydrate myself there seeing her enjoy the landscape, she did not even notice that I looked at her, she was totally focused on the show, created by her, while I enjoyed watching her, enjoying that extreme fascination.

Chapter 4. The revelations

Year 2017

I woke up abnormally excited. My body was still shaking from the sexual derby the day before. We had made love full steam ahead. It was a festive Monday. So I decided to go out onto the balcony from where you could appreciate a tiny piece of the sea, shining brightly with each ray of sunlight.

That was enough to enjoy a cup of Coatepec coffee, well loaded, and continue reading that fascinating book about the universe.

I felt pressured to finish it as quickly as possible. On each page I found a revelation of things that would be beneficial in my life.

Alternately I was reading another book that had given me some answers on how to deal with this pain from two years ago.

I was 20 pages away from finishing the book "Descartes' error" by Damasio. He was understanding how the brain, emotions, feelings worked. For many scientists, the brain, mind, and body are one. They cannot be separated as we have always thought, they act together. Like for Hawking, in The Theory of Everything, in the universe everything is linked. In human beings there is an indivisible connection of body, brain and mind.

But above all I was impressed to know that for most theorists there were three entities united in oneself, without division, in the decision-making of our lives: the body, the brain and the mind.

All my life I believed that we were like a processor. We had hardware with all the necessary utensils to be able to operate like every limb and part of our body, a memory to record all the information acquired from birth to death and software to process at will of every action we did.

Shit!

I even thought that we were like a programmer made by a higher entity, an alien race watching over us from afar, as well as known computers, and that they systematically assembled us as if there were a superior race.

Never! God would always be above this species overseeing everything because he is greater than the greatest.

Perhaps this is how I imagined heaven, the Creator conducting an orchestra of brilliant minds, designing the best elements to create humans, giving them an extraordinary brain of which we only use 20 percent of their capacity, and providing us with body, strong hardware, to face any external obstacle, with the advantage of making it more armored. But two elements remain in all this: the soul and the mind.

If I were a boy studying first in high school, with the intention of going out to see my teenage girlfriend, I would say that they are the same, but from there I started to think differently. The mind is made up of what the body and brain live on a daily basis, but the soul is there. I thought it was like a ticket with no destination, and each one chooses, based on their experience, which path to take, but what about the soul? Does it exist? Or is it just the food of so many religions and cults?

I was besieged by all those questions until sitting on the balcony of my house passed that hateful neighbor, who felt Catalan and as much as I tried to avoid it he shouted at me:

- Neighbor, how are you? How does it feel to have won the classic and lost the league?

I was not a big fan of soccer, but as a child I grew up watching Hugo Sánchez, the top scorer in the most important league in the world in the biggest team of the time. At that time I was proud to be a Real Madrid fan. Real Madrid became an icon of my happiness during my childhood. I only had to answer.

-Neighbor, even if they win the next 20 leagues and all the Champions will stay light years away from us.

-We'll catch up, neighbor, don't worry.

-It doesn't worry me in the least - I blurted out that somewhat macho rhetoric, but it came out of my soul. - Neighbor would be easier if you were meringue. You live in error. Even Shakira lives in deception. She thinks she is happy with Piqué, but, imagine, if she had met Sergio Ramos, she would not have a son, but rather like 25 kids. He is the greatest and fiercest defender on earth, but she chose the first one she found instead of a real man. Imagine being the defense of a weak team, to be the tower of the team that attack the most and world champion. No neighbor, don't get confused, there are men to men.

With that, the neighbor had to go into his house spitting word and a half, while continuing with my reading.

Lecture four was the most exciting. I could stay without eating, without sleeping, without looking at the sunlight, but I wanted to know what the magic was that encompassed black holes.

I was devouring at the same rhythm the lines of that book, the popcorn and my American coffee. Excited, I was discovering details that I did not know about the universe, in fact, I did not understand most of the concepts specifically, but in general, each chapter was foolproof, since as I did not know everything about these topics, I managed to have an overview of what Hawking wanted to convey and bequeath to the world.

Apparently, before his death, Hawking was unable to determine if his famous Cygnus X-I was a black hole, but he left the challenge to his colleagues.

I was surprised to read, for example, that "*a black hole could drive ten large power plants, just by taking advantage of their emission.*" That could be an inexhaustible source of energy for our planet.

Although reading the options I saw it impossible at this time. "*And the only way to put it into orbit around the earth would be to lure it there, towing a large mass in front of it, akin to putting a carrot in front of the donkey. It doesn't seem like a very practical proposition, at least not in the immediate future.*" But not even that I stopped thinking about the possibility of returning to her, returning time, space. At times I analyzed my thoughts and felt I was going a little crazy every day when reading that complex book, but more to miss her.

And the conference ended like this: "*If we have not yet managed to find a prime black hole, there is general agreement that if we did, it would have to be emitting many gamma rays and x-rays. If we find one, I will win the Nobel Prize."* And yes, he passed away without having the black hole, nor the Nobel Prize.

I cut the reading a bit to prepare something to eat. I put a little of each vegetable dish stored in the refrigerator on a plate and sprinkled with vinaigrette and enough salt. Through the window you could smell the rich aroma of fried bananas and listen to the characteristic sound they make when smoking. My mouth was watery, but I didn't plan to waste time going out to buy that craving. I had to continue on my way to her.

I began to devour the salad overflowing with lettuce, seaweed, spinach, peanuts, almonds, arugula, and chard, while drinking coffee to satisfy myself and continuing to amaze me with Hawking's revelations, especially by a statement in his fifth lecture.

"It would be very difficult to explain why the universe should have started precisely in this way, except as the act of a God who wanted to create beings like us. One of the greatest scientists in our history speaking of God, but above all accepting that the universe was like a perfect space created for us human beings. The laws do not tell us what the universe was like when it started, it would still be God's will to wind the clock and choose how it started."

Everything was so complex. The universe seemed like a place designed by laws so complex that no human, no matter how Hawking, could discern a whole. In the reflection a cough attacked me for drinking the coffee quickly. I went out for a moment to the balcony, to breathe some fresh air, and see the sea. So much perfection in the world questioned me.

If you were God would you leave a manual on how to create the world? That would be like leaving the power to create humanity to anyone.

If he is a supreme being, can the human mind understand something as high as his creation?

Suddenly, a roar was heard in the kitchen, just as I was asking those questions about God. I had never questioned divine things, I was afraid it sounded like blasphemy. I ran into the house, but the windows were closed. The first thing I saw was a painting on the floor, the one that adorned the main wall, she and I portrayed the day we met at a popular party.

Chapter 5. Making history

Year 2005

I never imagined that I would care so much about February 15, however, the first years together served as a reference to never forget that date. I always looked forward to it and it ended up becoming the most special day of my life.

We lived in the same city, Coatzacoalcos, in the state of Veracruz, south of the Gulf of Mexico, where even the waves of the sea are warm throughout the year. We had never met in a small municipality.

That Sunday in February was no exception. The rays of the sun announced spring. The hangover from celebrating "Valentine's Day" the previous Saturday had left me exhausted.

But I could not miss my highest duty as a Catholic, attend midday mass. I had a hydrating drink in a jiffy to make up for lost fluids and keep my mouth dry.

There were more people than usual in the church. Apparently it was a celebration of some saint. The temple was carefully decorated, in many bright colors, and on the outskirts were typical food stalls and folk dances were performed.

When I was a child, the moment of Communion during mass was my favorite. Not because I received Holy Communion very often, but it was a sign of the nearness of the end of the Sunday ceremony. With the merciless hangover and my head about to explode, seeing all the parishioners stand up to receive Communion was a sign of relief. It never crossed my mind to stop and do the same. Not because I did not want to, but I had been without confession for several years, and taking into account the remorse of the previous night, where I would have probably exceeded all pleasures, it was unthinkable to take the sacred body of Christ after that blessed revelry.

I saw all the known families of the city go to the line and receive the Host, some greeted me from afar: the Martínez, the Álvarez, the Robles, the Vera, the López, the Hernández, the Fernández, the González, the Rosado, the Ramos. As in any small city, families line up in long lines, from the entrance to the pulpit, with their sons and daughters wearing their most elegant costumes, some of them less covered by the intense heat. Several of those beautiful young women had been part of my life. How good those stories would go with me to my grave, even though I wanted to repeat them.

Suddenly, I felt like I could stop the world. That innocent girl looking at the lectern was totally unknown to me. Would she be foreign and would be visiting our city? I could not find another explanation for her to have gone unnoticed. I calculated her 23 gleaming springs. She wore a typical Jarocha costume. Her beauty was enhanced. The brilliance of her eyes looked challenging, combined with a cut very close to the waist and a skirt with non-traditional openings, improvised by some local artist. Go irreverence, show half a leg in full Communion. As much as I tried to meet her gaze, she just floated down the hall until she left the room.

I felt my head explode. I left the church heading home to continue sleeping, after I had already lost sight of the beautiful jarocha, who was surely heading to her home. The exit was slow, because of so many people walking slowly through the food stalls and typical sweets installed on the sidewalk. On the way I greeted a couple of friends, of whom I rejected the invitation to go to dinner that night at the boardwalk. All I wanted was another head and a hammock.

As I could, I slipped away. I was one step away from turning the corner, to walk faster, to my house, when I caught a glimpse of a typical costume similar to that of the mysterious parishioner. It could be someone else, I thought.

The closer I got, my mind was damaged by last night's alcohol consumption and I could think of the words to mediate a conversation. It was her, asking the street vendor for a coconut. I stopped pretending to buy one. She was impassive, mute, already preparing my coconut. She put Valentina sauce, "Miguelito", "Chamoy", "Tajín" and lemon.

Desire won me and I had the courage to slyly release her:

      -Gastritis is included. - She smiled and responded to the boat soon.

      -Do you know a trusted gastroenterologist in the city?

I already knew that script. It had worked for me on dozens of occasions. Without looking down, I took a card out of my wallet and said:

      -Of course, Dr. Juan Martín Vaamonde Pontevedra to serve you.

Gently she took the card and put it in her embroidered black handbag.

-Aurora, Aurora Bessi, great pleasure. - She answered extending her hand, and instantly accelerated my bloodstream, creating a vacuum in my stomach almost on the verge of vomiting by hangover.

-My pleasure. When you need a consultation or an American coffee, I am at your service.

-I will take it into account, but I only drink espresso, the American is for weak stomachs or brave gastroenterologists knowing that any discomfort themselves can be cured.

- Done! An epresso, when?

-I don't know, my father is a sailor, and he has to know who I'm dating. Also, extremely jealous. I don't think you can deal with it.

-I have no problem with that. It will only be an espresso.

-Okey, doctor, I'll leave you my number. Send me a message and I'll check the available time in my schedule.

Aurora wrote her number down on a piece she cut from my business card and hurried off to where her parents were waiting for her.

I was so excited that when I got home I told my parents what had happened. They did not pay attention to me because they thought it would be one more romance in my life. They had lived with me all my idylls, both disappointments and joys.

I lay down to sleep to finish with the hangover and the fatigue; however, something did not let me stick my eyelids. I was like this for a couple of hours, trying to fall asleep, but there was a volcano erupting in my mind, telling me over and over, "Send her a message, send her a message." I was dying to know more about her, but I knew, by the unwritten rules, that sending her a message soon would be evidence of interest and submission, so I got tangled up in the sheets again and tried to sleep.

Damn! It was useless. I took my cell phone and wrote that line with nerves tickling my body, almost as if I had it in front of me. *"Espresso tomorrow at 6 pm?"* I felt a relief when I sent it, the pressure dropped, I relaxed, and I was able to fall asleep, waiting for her response.

Chapter 6. Last conferences

Year 2018

That day a photo frame was dropped out of nowhere and exploded to pieces on impact on the floor. It was only the glass and the frame that broke. The photo was still intact. So I went to find another frame in the closet to put in the kitchen. Aurora spent much of her time cooking for me, indulging in all sorts of gastronomic varieties that she learned on television.

I thought of a rebuke from God for the fall of the painting, for having dared to question him, and for not having attended church that Sunday. It also crossed my mind that she had been there in spirit at that moment. I closed Hawking's book leaving the separator at the beginning of the sixth conference, and dressed casually to go to church, even if it was at the end of mass. I wanted to feel at peace.

Listening to the priest's sermon reassured me, although he spoke of eternal life, but I thought of an infinite life with her.I left mass walking quickly, while some tears came up as I passed by the place where we met looks, words and laughter for the first time.

I spent almost an hour sobbing in the chair, until drinking a black tea to calm my emotions to continue reading Hawking.

The sixth conference talked about the direction of time and kept surprising me more and more. It seemed like I was reading a science fiction novel and not a science book.

Those questions gave hope to my life. Would you see broken glasses put on the floor and jump onto the table? Would they be able to remember tomorrow's prices and make a fortune on the Stock Market? It might seem somewhat academic to worry about what will happen when the universe collapses again, as it will not contract for at least 10 billion years. But there is a faster way to find out what will happen: jumping into a black hole. In the contraction phase people would live their lives in reverse. They would die before birth. They would grow younger as the universe contracted. This idea is attractive because it would create a nice symmetry between the expansion and contraction phases.

I did not think about this nonsense of taking advantage of knowing what would happen to accumulate wealth. I was looking for an alternative to avoid her departure. At that time, the concept of black holes seemed like that formula to see her again.

I went to pour myself another coffee in the kitchen. That day I did not plan to sleep until reading the last page of that enigmatic book. I also opened a bottle of wine, cut some pieces of cheese and accompanied them with some grapes to make the evening more pleasant.

The seventh conference was titled "The Theory of Everything" and the conclusion was a defeat for science to unify in a theory what God had created. Hawking ended by accepting that it was necessary to advance in partial fairs and not in a single theory, whose search has been called "unification of physics"

"However, it seems that the uncertainty principle is a fundamental characteristic of the universe in which we live."

For believers, like me, we call uncertainty God's design. So I let a university professor of statistics know when he asked about the definition of chance. I almost repeated the semester for that simple assertion and making an enemy of a scientist, whose ego was the size of the world. Fortunately, my career was medicine and I never heard from him again.

What a jerk! Not for doubting the existence of God, but for being subjective in his way of evaluating, putting the beliefs of a student before him. There were things that seemed too high for very select coefficients.

"When infinity is subtracted from infinity, the answer can be anything you want."

His statements were sometimes logical and made us see the paradigmatic limitations that we humans have that we only believe what fits our thoughts.

"We only see the three spatial and temporal dimensions in which space-time is flat."

The conclusion of the work left me with enough doubts to believe in a tomorrow with her. I had a hard time understanding how a black hole could do magic and possible things that human beings did not understand and yet it was the bet of science.

I felt like when I didn't understand how a computer works, how a chip could process information and even make decisions like a human mind. Everything in a small circuit, as if it were a kind of article that transforms everything into magic and creates new things.

Nor did I need to understand how pre-programmed planes work. Today is the time to fly alone, and yet I had used them to cross oceans and see a thousand places and I did not have to understand everything related to science. I just had to do like when I get home: turn on the switch and the magic begins to flow. So I just had to find out how to take advantage of cosmological science to try to see her again.

How would it work? I did not care. I just wanted that magic.

"There may be a theory of everything or we are just chasing a mirage. There seem to be three possibilities.1.- There really is a complete unified theory, which we will discover someday if we are intelligent enough.2.- There is no ultimate theory of the universe, but only an infinite sequence of theories that describe the universe with increasing precision.3.- There is no theory of the universe. Events cannot be predicted beyond a certain measure, but occur in a random and arbitrary way.

Can God make a stone so heavy that He cannot lift it? "

And I reached the last line, after hours of sleeplessness reading and writing down every detail in my notebook to be able to investigate concepts that could generate a way of seeing her.

"If we find the answers to it, it would be the triumph of human reason, because then we would know the mind of God."

I would never try to know the mind of God. That option didn't even cross my mind. I just cried daily every night, begging Him for a single opportunity, one more minute with her, at whatever cost. Just give me one more minute to talk to her, just 60 seconds, I have rehearsed word by word what I would say in that short time.

I just wanted you to know,
before I lose you again,
that you will always be in my dreams,
take them with you wherever you go.

The dreams of a life with you are always,
those of knowing every corner of the world with you
my mind will never be anywhere else
I give you my whole life
until the moment that God decides
From the first ray of light
until the last of the afternoon

You will stay forever
I will never lose you from my sight, from my body
You will be in every cubic millimeter of air
circulate through my lungs
In every milliliter through my veins,
you will be part of me
every day, every moment.

Forgive me for blinking a second and lose you

,At that moment I died too.

00:00:59

Chapter 7. The wedding

Year 2007

It was too coincidental to a certain extent that when I told her to choose a place to get married she had thought of the same place that me. I did not mention it from the beginning because I wanted to please her and perhaps for her this place was not so attractive, she probably already had a place where she dreamed of walking down the aisle.

We had the facility of not having guests, so it would be very easy to choose the place without the location being a problem for the arrival of friends. Fortunately, we could also afford at that time a trip to any part of the world. I thought of the first option that I would choose the Notre Dame Cathedral in Paris, because it is the capital of love. Besides that it was one of the majestic buildings on the planet. I also remembered hearing her say that knowing the Florence Cathedral was one of her longings. It was the fascination of both of us, although we were not fortunate enough to get to know that white, green and pink work of art together.

Another option for both was the Madrid Cathedral. In Mexico, the Basilica of Guadalupe could be the most hackneyed, but also the most important site.

We chose a historical and emblematic place. We both agreed it would be something very romantic and original, although it was not ostentatious to marry in a humble church, whose tradition was that it was the first one in America, La Antigua, Veracruz, which was also the first city council of our continent. There we spent several hours together, eating by the river while the afternoon fell on some occasions when we traveled for work reasons to the state capital.

The Villa Rica de la Vera Cruz was founded there, which was later transferred to another location. Hernán Cortes lived there. We had the opportunity to be in that extensive hacienda, which was his house, now in ruins. There we decided on March 6 to found our life together, as ourselves and to undertake the rest of our days. It did not have the elegance or magnitude of Notre Dame Cathedral, almost the same age. On the contrary, it was very rustic and of a very small size. Its white color matched perfectly with her dress. I think there were several criteria that led her to choose it. We had both been there, enjoying those landscapes. We were neighbors of that land. It was very original. We had never heard of any sacrament in that place.

We went to great lengths to adorn the construction, with vintage details to match the wood and walls. We put a path of roses and flowers through each corner of the church. At the entrance of the enclosure we place floral decorations on the walls and on the wood of the door. The small garden around it we can and we put on the fence that surrounded the place ribbons the color of wood.

She chose a simple wedding dress, but it highlighted her beauty and every part of her body. She even had an opening that showed her thin white legs. A slight neckline showed her youth and beauty. She was not wearing a veil. We do not consider it necessary. We wanted something modern, but above all made to measure, wishes and beliefs.

Seeing her walk safely and happily, step by step, slowly, through that anteroom of roses, until she reached me at the altar, was an exciting wait. My body shuddered, thinking that nothing could separate us anymore. It was the most exciting and nervous moment in my life. I had a great responsibility, from that moment, which was inalienable, once sworn before God: that of making her happy.

It was just her and me in worship. So we both took care of the details, first I gave her the golden coins representing the livelihood that I would be for our family. Then there was the long tie, which the father helped to place us in the absence of a quorum. Finally, the rings where we accepted each other forever, with the inscription on each of this date and a phrase written by both. I placed it on her index finger, adding to the litany some phrases of my inspiration, then she did the same without saying anything, just sticking to the traditional instructions.

It was a brief celebration, but very solemn and too emotional. The father's sermon was dedicated to wishing us immense happiness and many blessings, he even gave us a rosary and still gave us a couple of gossip about marriage stories.

After two years of relationship, with so many obstacles overcome, we finally fulfilled our desire to be together, despite everything and everyone.

One day, without imagining it, everything went against our relationship. We never understood why, if our love was pure. We had a theory that we were too loved by our families and so they did not get used to the idea that someone might deserve to be with us.

We decided to separate ourselves from the world we knew and start our own. It was very painful for both of us to get away from the people we loved the most, but it was a commitment we made to start from scratch and not drag those problems into the relationship. We believed in advance that it would only be temporary and that we would be sitting at a large table again, and happy to tell anecdotes and details of the wedding.

Chapter 8. Souls

We are souls. It is a universally known truth. We have always accepted that premise seen from any religion, although no one has proven it. No one has scientific evidence of the existence of the soul.

That abstract entity is considered the essence of each person, of which there is not even a consensus of probable existence or definition. It is only believed to give meaning to our lives. It seems to be something deeper than thought, emotion, or feeling. The soul is usually located between the body and the mind. The mind was the intangible result of what the brain, physically called neurons, and body could create. Many authors attributed the characteristics of the soul to the mind. There were so many things to understand: mind, brain, feelings, thoughts, emotions, and to all this add the material part, universe, atoms, relativity, gravity, temperature, space, time. It made me anxious to think about so many things and even more that I didn't know about it.

Nor was I clear what the correct conceptual sedition of the soul was, and so I explorative decided to obtain some information to give a little scientific rigor to my research, but not consulting experts, but with ordinary human beings.

At night, when I was leaving work, I carried out a simple survey. I needed to have information, even if it was exploratory, about this concept for my unknown.

On the way home, I stopped by an express to the Italian coffee shop, which kept me awake for an hour to read before falling asleep. I entered the place and took the first table by the way.

-Miss, excuse me, what is the soul for you? - I asked the young woman who took my order. For an instant she was surprised. She did not understand the question. I clarified that it was only a questioning to test the knowledge that people had about that concept.
- I don't know- she replied as she teased, thoughtfully, feeling pressured. -I can't find words at the moment, sir; I'm busy tending the tables.

Her gaze was like that of a deer frightened by the roars of the forest and I tried to make her understand that it was irrelevant.

-Yes, excuse me, it's something unimportant - I told her to forget the matter.

-Well, I think it is that part of us that we cannot see, but that makes us be - she surprised me with her response and earned me a smile of admiration.

-There is no exact answer, it was just to know what people think about this topic. Can you serve me another espresso? - I said to try to break the ice and forget the subject.

-Yes, of course - she answered and retired to the kitchen.

Right at the next table were two young girls, so close to me that I overheard the conversation about love affairs. But when I questioned the young waitress about the soul, both were attentive to the answer, as that topic caught their attention. So I looked at each one and kindly asked for their opinion as well, but I interrupted their conversation. Both agreed.

-The soul? - Asked the tall blonde, about 27 years old, whose conversation hours ago was agony for not being sure if she loved her boyfriend or not. Now she had a deeper question. -The soul is the mind and it is where you allow many things to enter. In a few words the thought - she added very surely, in a pragmatic way, while she drank a bit of a frothy cappuccino and looked at her dark-skinned, voluptuous body friend, questioning her with her eyes.

-The soul is what we have in the body and when we die it goes away, since we are only a recipient - was the girl's response, blushing, as if waiting for acceptance or rejection.

Both had a similar concept, although it was not scientifically proven.

-Thank you very much, girls, excuse the interruption - I said, but not before mentioning the real reasons that intrigued me to know your concept of soul.

I immediately went to the bathroom, while continuing with my qualitative study.

It was almost eight at night, when an elegant lady entered the place. I calculated 34 years. I couldn't miss the opportunity to ask her. She looked polite and educated. Her response was as expected.

-The soul is like the energetic memory that contains the information of what you have to work on in this life in order to evolve.

Her response blew me away. I expected something different, but it made me deepen my personal concept of the soul.

When I was about to say goodbye, she elaborated on other words that I was slow to understand but that I wrote down quickly on my cell phone.

-But the soul is contained in the body. When the soul dies it has a chance to return to the source.

-Thank you very much - I said.

I went into the bathroom and started washing my hands. A young man did the same. I took the opportunity to survey him, but not before explaining that it was for a qualitative study and did not think I was courting him. Who polls another man in the anteroom of the urinals?

-It's the weight you feel when you don't feel anything else - was his reply.

I finished cleaning up quickly and left the bathroom, making the corresponding notes.

What a complex and profound subject! Most people were a little intimidated when expressing their concepts on the subject.

I decided to stay in the cafeteria until 10 at night, when the place was closed, so that I could question more people.

A family came to another table. A young couple and their two girls. As they order, the older of them saw me typing on my cell phone in a hurry. She asked me in his tender voice:

-What do you do?

-My homework - I answered so she understood that I was busy.

- Can I help you? - She said in her small voice. I thought about saying no and turning abruptly, but I didn't want to be impolite, least of all with a child. So I took advantage of the detail to investigate from another perspective. Children have a great imagination.

- Sure. Look, I am doing a survey of all the people that I consider intelligent and in this case I have selected you to answer this question, what is the soul for you?

Maybe the girl had no idea what I was questioning, but surprisingly she gave me the answer, while looking at me with her innocent face and big, blue eyes:

-Eternity.

The little girl smiled and returned to her table. How could a creature of maximum 10 years have that vision of these spiritual questions?

I wrote that answer down on my mobile and looked around at who else might be a candidate for my question.

There was a table in front of me, with a couple who had observed my little research exercise. So I felt confident approaching them to ask if they could also answer that question. They gladly accepted. It was a couple that radiated joy. It reminded me of when Aurora and I drank coffee and laughed all the time.

- The soul is everything to me - replied the handsome young man named Osvaldo, as he put his arm around his girlfriend's neck as a sign that it was her turn.

-For me, the soul is our signature in the universe. It is the other opportunity to live in the universe - was Maria's response. He brought me ideas that turned my unconscious.

I said goodbye to them thanking them and wishing them great happiness together, forever.

I returned to my table while another interview possibility presented itself. There were few diners left because the place was about to close and most were families accustomed to not interrupting the family time of laughter with the children, and who considered the moments to share bread and salt sacred.

I decided better to change from an experimental place to a more informal and crowded place at that time. Next to the cafeteria there was a small bar called "Guavinas", traditional in style. So I opted to change the aroma of the coffee for the bitter taste of a dark beer, very cold.

That night I remembered Hawking's concepts of the stars and thought about the immensity of that dark sky, while observing a majestic full moon, and felt the sea breeze on my cheeks. I sat at the center of three tables for a chance to ask different people. Unlike the cafeteria, they were more homogeneous groups, in terms of age and sex.

On my right side, a group of young women, one of whom was trying to flirt with me, but when I raised my right hand she saw my wedding ring and without wanting I made her give up that task. I never thought to take that ring off. My oath at the altar was to be Aurora's husband all my life and I planned to fulfill that promise.

One of those women, who seemed to be the life of the party, who already had a few extra glasses, started talking to me and humming a song from The Cure sublimely mixed by the night's disc jockey.

-It's my favorite song from The Cure - the girl was shouting in my ear. I felt her breath full of rum.

-Mine too, "Pictures of you", mixed, it sounds incredible - I shouted back.

-Yes, it gives it a little more intensity.

Every time she answered me, she got closer to my right ear so that I could hear her, due to the volume of the music and also because drunk people believe that they have to speak louder.

-And your wife? - she asked when she saw my ring.

-It's a long story - I told her not to go into details and ruin her joy with sad stories, however, she turned her chair to face me.

-I have all night to hear your story. My name is Claudia, and you? She had a nice smile, similar to my younger sister's. I started to tell her the whole long story and why I was there at the bar at the time, instead of being with Aurora making love to her like every night. The good thing about having a conversation with the leader of the group of friends was that after giving me her answer, she began to support me by questioning her numerous companions.

-For me, the soul is connectivity between heaven and earth - was one of the responses found in this group of people.

It focused my thought on Aurora. It was what I needed, a connection between heaven and earth, between the divine and the mortal to reach her.

- Sounds crazy, right?

-I like it - I replied and I shook my beer with her glass of rum with mineral water, as a sign of approval and celebration for her response.

I questioned all her friends and other people in the bar and the most frequent answer was "essence". More than half of my respondents used it alone or accompanied by some other concept. Hence the most used words were in the following order: "spirit", "immortal", "inner me", "the abstract, what you do not see", "my identity", "what makes me unique and unrepeatable" and "Energy".

And from there I could find a great variety of answers with different words, but always having concepts in common.

"The purest of being". "Protection". "It is what identifies each person and makes them different and full of love." "The soul is like the spark that ignites an engine, what people remember of us beyond our face or body." "What comes from the heart." "Our intrapersonal record." "It is a state of matter that reflects our being." "Well, I think it is an abstract entity that inhabits all people and gives it the capacity to feel." "The beginning of our life and freedom." "It is an abstract part that constitutes the human body." "The soul is where the joys or sorrows are deposited in our day to day." "The soul is what allows us to communicate with God." "A part of the vessel of infinite darkness with sparks of light." "It is what gives us life." "The deepest part of being". "The fire inside".

Even the boy who sold cigarettes and gum outside the bar gave me his definition. To close my survey, I went to my house while feeling the cool night wind and meditating on the subject.

We all believe we have a soul, but we have never seen one. The theory that its weight is 21 grams is derived from the estimation of the weight lost by a body after dying.

Perhaps it is that bond between us and the world, time, space. I got home and drank some mezcal with an orange, while trying to find in each drop of alcohol consumed an answer to understand the fate of souls, but more specifically the fate of her soul. It was the only thing important to me.

Ideas kept popping up in my head. When astronauts travel to outer space they carry special equipment to protect themselves. Nobody would withstand the high or low temperatures of outer space, pressure, gravity or lack of oxygen.

And back to Hawking's question, what was there before the Big Bang? Let's think for a moment about those theories of microscopic living beings that later evolved until they reached homo sapiens. To also believe that microorganisms were suddenly developing is like thinking about the certainty of the rejected theory of spontaneous generation.

Another idea overwhelming my mind was how we could think of being the only thinking beings in the universe, where the earth and we were a tiny part. A very egotistical theory of man.

I took another sip of the mezcal and the acidity of the orange made me shudder and keep thinking about situations that I hadn't seen before. If he were the creator of the universe, just as an assembler does by designing a perfect computer, the most essential part, which in this case could be the soul, would cover it very well so that no external agent could harm it. This is how we design computers, they have a memory, a processor and hardware that covers and protects these important parts from external factors such as rain, heat, humidity, shock, human contact. The heart supplies electrical energy to that computer, in the same way that a computer has its power source to turn it on or off, something like the air we breathe.

And yet the perfect computer has a heart and a brain, but not a soul. It has a power source that gives energy and an information processor, but the union of these elements can never create something similar to the soul description that humans have generated. So maybe they will always be machines.

At the time, those comic strips of machines with artificial intelligence, taking over the world and exterminating the human race, seemed like a fallacy. The only one who could eliminate the man was the man himself.

And back to the point, if you or I who read this testimony could create a perfect civilization, how would we do it?

We would design the adequate protection, resistant, but sensitive to any change that could threaten the essence of each being.

Human skin has those characteristics. It protects us from fire or extreme cold, sends the signal to the brain of needs and dangers, and even suffers damage before jeopardizing the entire internal part of this perfect machine.

And we would think of a place to store all those experiences that are forming learning and developing the way to evolve and subsist. That organ would be similar to the brain.

We would also need a source of power that encourages all activities, such as the heart, beating non-stop day and night to keep the body on, without disconnecting for a single moment.

God's model is perfect. Nothing and nobody could have created something as perfect as the human being, a body where to protect the essence of each person.

God did not create only man or woman; He did something deeper, the essence of each entity anywhere. He designed an immortal soul that can reincarnate not only in time, but in space. It can be maintained so that you can stay and wait another time.

So looking at various evidences I decided to formulate my own theory of everything, which would encompass everything we know in the world, the material and the spiritual.

Chapter 9. The goodbye

Year 2015

That year was an ordeal. I was facing the most disastrous battle of my life. She and I fought with that intruder lodged in her body, destroying every organ and dream in the future.

Until then, this disease had seen her from the sidelines. She had no acquaintances who suffered from this disease. So when we went to the doctor and found out she had cancer, I was absorbed. It's like listening to a death sentence. I cried, I screamed, I lost the will to live, just thinking of her absence, however, she never cried or implored. She always fought like a warrior.

This was Aurora: brave, able to face any circumstance or pain for being together. I thought that a relationship reaches a climax when you can no longer love anymore, that it reaches a peak, however, discovering an Aurora fighting against the world's deadliest enemy, for our love, made me love her in an inexplicable, unmatched way , not earthly.

We started visiting other doctors to receive more opinions, to take treatments, from the most complex to the homemade ones.

There is no place more distressing than the waiting room of a hospital. The cold of the place increases fear due to the uncertainty of something that is imminent. I only hoped for a favorable or lethal response. That night I sensed it. I saw it on her tired face from fighting. I encouraged her from the first rays of dawn until she closed her eyes at night so that she would not abandon me, that she had the strength to resist and live one more day, and with that I was happy, even though we could no longer go for a walk, touch the palms of our feet on the wet sand of the beach, as in our glory days. Or drink coffee while watching the sublime sunset over the sea and the hills. There I was, as usual, sitting for hours, drinking coffee, walking around the chairs while watching the seconds go by.

Calvary was the same. It had become more frequent. At first it was once a month and suddenly every 15 days, then every week. Three days before we had been there, I still had pain in my body for having spent the whole night sleeping between two benches. I saw her very weak, barely and could speak. I took her to emergencies. Her face had never been so pale. The nurses and doctors quickly realized the severity. They put her on a stretcher and entered immediately. Before I could kiss her parched lips and tell her that I loved her forever.

That moment was eternal. I felt everything run in slow motion, staying with the sensation of her lips. Her body was lost when the door to the room closed and I had nothing more to wait. I felt so fragile in that instant. I was just crying non-stop, leaning against the railing of the stairs that held me so I wouldn't faint with pain, trying to stammer out some prayer to invoke a supreme power to heal her.

I was short of breath and would go out to breathe a little bit in the parking lot, then buy some candy from the mobile stands outside the hospital and return to the ward. The clock said 11:50. In ten minutes and it would be May 29, and we would have survived one more day.

I leaned back on the empty benches and tried to get some rest. I fell sound asleep.

- Hello my love - I was awakened by her unmistakable voice.

- Aurora? How do you feel? - I replied. I had not seen her flushed cheeks for months, full of life. I felt an electric shock in my body. The blood in my veins was an incessant throbbing that quickened my heart.

-Better than ever, baby.

Her words charged my body with energy.

- You have no idea how happy it makes me see you like that. - I said, stuttering from my nerves at seeing her full of life.

-It makes me immensely happy to know that you have always been there for me.

-I always will, baby. I want to go home to pamper you in everything. I was greatly relieved. I had spent a year watching her decline day by day, lose strength, desire to live, but at that moment it seemed that the worst was over. We had defeated that monster that had taken over her body and her blood.
- Let's go! - She said in a voice of great optimism. It gave me energy.

I didn't feel the least bit tired after spending the night hunched over on the bench.

-Perfect! What room are you in to go get your things? - I said to her as she took my hand and hugged me tightly and kissed me on the lips.

- I'm in room 127, but I'm not taking anything.

-Why Baby? I must pick up your wedding ring and your chain with your mother's crucifix. Wait for me here. Sit down for a moment. I'm going for them.

-No dont go. Take me Home.

I was so happy to see her replenished to live longer.

-As you say. What I most want is for us to be home.

-I want to be at home, on every wall, in every window, in every corner, always by your side.

-Me too.- I held her hand tight and we headed for the exit. That victory ritual was similar to the one we did when we walked down the altar together.

I felt that instead of walking towards the exit we floated like that moment in which we united our lives. I turned to see her and her face was imprinted on my pupils. I saw her smile as when at our wedding she pulled my neck hard to kiss me.

For a moment everything was paralyzed. The noise of the loudspeakers calling some doctor was heard more and more tenuous. The air felt icy cold. The floor cleaner scent moved on to the flowery scent she used. The people around us seemed to look at us happy and smiling. Her lips tasted indescribable. But that moment could baptize it as the taste of Aurora's kisses, slightly sweet, which goes deep into the body until it completely bristles.

That's the way it was every time she kissed me. As I closed my eyes, my body seemed to collapse. I felt it heavy, tired, sore from the awkward position I was in. My neck was killing me with pain; I could barely open my eyes. Both legs were so numb that I couldn't put them on the floor from that electrifying tickle.

I sat motionless, physically devastated, and happy to see her one more time as a tall bearded doctor approached me. He asked me if I was related to Aurora Bessi.

I knew his words beforehand. I felt a merciless pain in my insides, but having seen her for the last time, happy and smiling, saying goodbye, vowing that she would live in every corner of the house, was enough not to burst into tears, although inside my heart was an ocean of tears. I was devastated. She had taken it. My heart was hers.

Chapter 10. The row

Year 2016

I was returning from a congress in Havana. I was tired from the hours of flight, coupled with a two-hour delay in takeoff and the forced wakefulness of the previous night with some fellow investigators of the event.

I drank various espresso. The first in the bar of the National Hotel, while waiting for the taxi that would take me to the airport. I took another espresso in the waiting room, waiting to pass the Immigration review. I had two more coffees.

Cuban coffee is for me one of the heritage of humanity. Its flavor is a delight. It also helped me wake up and not forget anything about packing in the suitcase, nor my official documents, nor my handbag.

In mid-flight, I drank another cup of coffee, but it was American. The difference with the Cuban is abysmal, but it was the only thing that stimulated my thinking. I felt a little nostalgic as I walked away.

In that hotel, the most symbolic of Havana and perhaps of the entire Cuban island, we had spent our honeymoon nine years ago. It was a whole week looking at the sea from the majestic garden hotel. Also appreciating sunrise, sunset, enjoying a mojito and watching her immaculate body sunbathe in a bathing suit. Seeing the show embraced in the hotel's own cabaret, "Parissien", was an unforgettable experience. Perhaps for that reason I agreed to attend that medical congress, to recreate happiness with her. So I didn't sleep last night. I drank a mojito, a daiquiri and a buccaneer beer, in that order, and smoked a number 4 Cohiba cigar, until it was two in the morning and I asked for the bill after expelling a couple of tears and going up my suitcase to leave the room.

Arriving in Mexico City in the high season is chaos. Several international flights arrived along with ours and there were crowds of people from the plane's departure gate. When I got to migration, there were rows going around and I couldn't even know where they started. Although the process was only a stamp in the passport and the queue was fast forward, more passengers from other flights constantly came down the escalators, mixing with the others.

A man in his 50s quickly got off and filtered through the lines until he reached almost a few meters from the migration module. Although many did not notice this action, some could observe how the passenger slipped between the lines to avoid queuing. I have never given much importance to these details, but I did not know that it was something very detestable by society. There were claims of all kinds. Ladies yelling at him that had questioned his education, one or two other men challenging him to the beat, others killing him with piercing glances and making him feel unfortunate. I even felt uncomfortable, since it was just a few people from me. Still one of the gentlemen who challenged him to blows continued to provoke him throughout the hall until the exit of the baggage check.

- It's not that bad. - I thought out loud.

-And who is getting you into this? - A man shouted at me with an umbrella in hand.

The truth is, he was right. I shouldn't be involved in his affairs, but I was really exaggerated by so much fuss. So seeing his eyes radiating fire, I decided to walk towards the airport exit to take a taxi.

-Excuse me - I said and continued on my way.

Obviously, there were also long lines at the taxi station, and when the nosy lord of the queue was about to form he was almost at the same height as me to form, but seeing his haste I let him pass. He looked quite nervous. He also looked impatient to leave the place. I did not care to leave the line or wait hours. I had nothing to do but arrive that Sunday at the hotel to sleep all day, recover and the next day continue my journey home.

So I didn't understand how someone put herself at risk just by saving herself a few minutes in line, regardless of running over others in her desire to go first. I didn't like that attitude, but I wasn't going to declare war on him either. I noticed I was sweating too much for the cool late winter day. My hands also trembled. I was worried about having him around, lest he was a serial killer or some deranged one. So I tried not to look at him to avoid looking for trouble. I just wanted to go to rest, have a relaxing tea in the softness of the sheets of that hotel on Avenida Obregón, where I would spend the night to travel very early the next day to my hometown, while listening to classical music, missing Aurora in every corner from my recently visited Hotel Nacional. The "mister hurries" took a cigar from the bag of his sack and turned to see me.

- Do you want a cigar? - He said, extending the pack of cigarettes to me.

-No, thank you very much, I don't smoke - I said. I didn't smoke, but I also wanted to cut off any conversation with him.

-An apology for a while ago. There are people who seem to be risking their lives and honor for not giving up a place in line.

-Yes. It's an exaggeration. So many people that we see walking and passing by on a daily basis and we judge them harshly without knowing their motives for doing unusual things.

-Well yes and more in this great city where millions of stories are woven every second - I said feigning empathy, but I still thought I was a disrespectful and daring lady.

-In my case, for example, I am working in the city of Monterrey and yesterday when I was about to leave work and attend the University stadium with my colleagues, I received one of the most unexpected and sad calls of my life. My wife Alicia suffered a sudden heart attack while doing housework. Can you imagine?

At that revelation, my face obviously changed and my attitude as well. He was right, how many times we go through life judging everyone, without really knowing the problems that are happening and that may be due mayor force.

I felt so bad that I had judged him and I even thought to tell the other guy who beat him to death before he boarded his taxi in another row located about 100 meters from where we were, but I thought it would be reliving a problem where there was no longer. Better I kept listening to that man.

-So sorry. I wish there was some way that people in our country were more civilized and understood without judging when a person really has a problem.

I really didn't know what to say anymore. I felt very sorry and at the same time identified with him for the great pain of his beloved, as happened to me, although in his case it was totally unexpected.

-And right now I am desperate because my two daughters, Kiara, 9, and Emil, 6, were left alone in the house for a long time until a neighbor realized the tragedy. They are with that neighbor because our entire family lives in Sinaloa. Imagine, my despair at the trauma of my daughters having witnessed the death of their mother, for not knowing how they are emotionally, for knowing if they are well. I want to come and take care of them, like their father that I am. It is something I do not wish on anyone. It is a very big frustration.

-I imagine it must be something very painful - was the only thing I managed to answer.

Knowing the reasons for this gentleman's anguish, I had no choice but to try to contribute something to dissipate his pain. Fortunately the young woman in front of him also heard the story and helped me convince all the passengers formed to yield to the mourner and to board the next taxi. I was greatly relieved by that little action taken to support him. I could not imagine the despair, as a parent, that it must feel to have children desperate for a tragic event.

I waited a few minutes while talking to the young woman ahead of me, and finally it was my turn.

I arrived at the hotel and despite the tea and music to relax, I could no longer sleep. My questioning was constant.

What happens to souls when people die?

Would the soul and spirit be the same as many people believe?

Some theories claim to remain in limbo floating, or in pain, or somewhere unknown.

Why are some good, others in pain, others perhaps demons?

What decides the role each essence plays in the ether?

Where do they rest and why do they rest?

It was at that moment that the image of the daring passenger who did not respect the line appeared involuntarily in my mind, with a totally valid but hidden justification only known to him.

And if, according to beliefs, the soul really reincarnates.

I envisioned all the possible alternatives, as I lay down on my bed to sleep. This time there was no bustle of hundreds of people forming, on the contrary, there were figures like gas tanks lined up. The smell was sometimes pleasant and unpleasant. Probably when someone dies, the scenario was similar, millions of souls from all over the world coming to concentrate in a place to wait to reincarnate and return to the face of the Earth.

What would that order be like?

Using logic, you could think of a long row ranked by various criteria. The main one, the date of death, the first to die will be the first to reincarnate.

Reincarnate in what?

In a person of the same or opposite sex, or in another living being, a plant, a bird, a fish, a horse, a worm. There were so many possibilities going through my troubled head. I felt the frequent stress of work. Thinking about these things really stressed me out. My neurons seemed to catch fire the more I thought about these spiritual issues. I needed professional help on these issues, and in my experience there were two places in the world, purely spiritual, magical cities. One of them, Catemaco, in the state of Veracruz, about 200 kilometers from my house, and that at least at the national level was an obligatory site on the subject. I met the other place in my university stage, on summer vacation. We traveled, with my friend Ankitt, kilometers of road to reach the Taj Mahal in the city of Agra in India. When I asked Ankitt about a special place in a country known for its beliefs and mysticism, he replied:

-The spiritual capital of India is Varanasi. It is a place in the north of the country bathed by the sacred waters of the Ganges River. If someday you have existential doubts there is no other place where you can dispel it.

Chapter 11. The honey moon

Year 2007.

There were only three days of rest that I could take from work after the wedding with Aurora. Although we had a life together, there was little time to enjoy together, however, we tried to think about it and enjoy every moment to the fullest.

The first day we went to Varadero. There in the crystalline waters of the Caribbean we kissed watching the sunset and making love very subtly so that no one around noticed it.

Fortunately at that time there were few tourists. It was a unique feeling. Her skin scraping my body with the sand, the sound of the wind on the waves causing a soft breeze combined with her agitation when moving fast, but hidden.

Her hands squeezing my back tight, while I looked at the sun on the horizon. The taste of her salty saliva made each kiss different. There were many combined and exciting sensations.

The combined smell of sand, her sweaty, salt-water bathed skin, and her perfume excited me more than ever, to the point of ending very soon. Feeling that touch of sand and her skin when I entered it, added to her orgasm, ended up stealing my breath.

I could barely get out of the sea. My legs were shaking, I felt them weak and relaxed. I barely touched the sand on the shore and vanished with it lying on my shoulder. I fell asleep I don't know how long. I only know that when I opened my eyes I did it driven by that feeling that someone is looking at you. And so it was, she watched me as my exhausted body regained strength.

-Sorry, Rory - that's what I said to you affection - was tired. I had to regain some energy.

-It seems perfect to me because you're going to need them all night - she said with a mischievous and perverted smile. She was laughing when I saw her.

It was already dark and we lay down in a hammock in the room we rented for the night. Enjoying the breeze, we stayed a few hours before retiring to the room.

I finished drinking a buccaneer beer and relaxed with a hug. The wind picked up a bit to move the hammock without having to pull it. It moved naturally like the waves of the sea. We hadn't taken off our bathing suits, but feeling her legs brushing my fingertips excited me. Her back was turned. I noted the effect of feeling and looking at her legs. She had practiced volleyball since she was a child and they were a soft rock at that time, their limbs exfoliated by the sand and sea salt. So, in that position, hugging her with her back touching my chest, I discovered a little my bathing suit. Hers there was no need, with a movement of my member the part of her bikini was slightly removed, allowing me to penetrate her without complications. I hugged her tighter kissing her back until I fainted with pleasure and tiredness on the hammock, and woke up with the first rays of the sun that burned my eyelids.

- The good thing we would make love all night - I heard in her recriminating voice.

Her ironic smile enchanted me, but now I was sorry that I had fallen asleep all night. It couldn't happen to me again. That day I drank a lot of coffee.

We have breakfast in the main garden of the hotel, which is on a hill surrounding the beach. The view that day was wonderful and the sun was shining brightly. The tan on her skin looked like a work of art. It was my perfect breakfast.

Her light green gaze shining brightly to the rhythm of the sun that caused other nuances. The soft, delicate skin of her hand caressing mine. The turquoise Caribbean sea in the background. A well-toasted bread, with a brown tone without reaching dark, smeared with fresh butter melting in my mouth. A Cuban espresso with two tablespoons of sugar.

The sound of the wind, the singing of birds, the waves enraged by the heat, the aroma of coffee, the bustle of tourists also eating breakfast around, were part of the ideal setting. Being with her was the most important and successful decision of my life.

We boarded a van that took us to the most important tourist destinations in Havana. El Capitolio, Old Havana. We went to the Bodeguita del Medio to drink mojitos. To Floridita to consume daiquiris, to El Morro bay to observe this impressive view from the highest part of the fortress. We take photos at each location. At night we went to the most important cabaret show: at El Tropicana. When we left that place it was already a little late. Despite my coffee rations, the weariness of the sun and walking through the historic center made me fall asleep back to the hotel.

She woke me up and guided me to the hotel room, but as I passed by the bar and listened to the sound of the waves I looked for more fight:

-Let's have a mojito while looking at the boardwalk.

- But you can barely stand up! - she questioned me.

-Don't worry with a Cuban coffee and a mojito we will solve it.

I drank a couple of sips from the coffee, we toasted a delicious mojito and ordered a number four cigar. She never smoked, but she wanted to feel that sense of freedom and security of cigar smokers.

- Now you are the commander of the Cuban revolution? - She mocked, as I hugged her. Just then a young man passed by selling green military caps as a souvenir and I bought her one.

-Of course! - I said as I put the cap on, smoked the cigar and immediately took a sip of the mojito. She asked me to pose for several photos. That selfie was meant for our living room because it summed up our happiness.

I fell asleep inside her. It was an indescribable feeling of communion. I noticed her orgasm and keep moving until I also imagine myself in the depth of her spirit and mind.

I pulled her towards me until she was lying on my chest. We do not talk. We could communicate mentally. She understood she wanted to spend the whole night like this.

Through the window you could see a full moon that was too bright. I put soft music on my cell phone.

On the last day of our honeymoon, when I went downstairs to the lobby I purposely forgot my cell phone in the room. I pretended not to have noticed and asked Aurora to come up for it while checking if Eduardo had already arrived, our tour guide, a very kind, friendly and accommodating guy, but with a small flaw, for everything he tried to be more kind to my wife, and complimented her. I saw him enter the lobby and he saw me too.

-Good morning, Juan Martín, how are you? - He said extending his hand to me.

-Excellent, thank God - I said without letting go of his hand and moving a little closer to his ear - Look, Eduardo, I don't know what they are like here in Cuba, but back in Mexico we killed the son of a bitch who called our wife beautiful . Do you understand

-Of course, man, one just tries to be nice, but you don't have to worry. I will not speak more than necessary.

-Perfect! By the way, I like you very much. You're a reasonable guy - I said as I patted him on the back for friendship and threatened at the same time.

I love when people understand things the good way, without going to extremes. That day was just as beautiful as the previous ones, with the variant that the guide now kept his healthy distance and tried to always be away from my Rory.

The sun was plummeting. Her days tanned skin looked spectacular. Not only I thought about it. There was no man who did not look away from her as she walked in the Plaza de la Revolución. She stood out among dozens of tourists from various countries. I kept taking photos of her, with the giant images, of background, of Fidel and Che Guevara.

- Eduardo, when does the baseball season start? - I asked our guide.

-It's mid-season. In fact, today the Industriales de La Habana play, the best team in the world.

-Hahaha. The same is true of the Warriors of the University of Sotavento, the team of my city.

-No, my lord. I'm serious. If you don't believe me, you can testify today that they are playing against the Santiago de Cuba team.

I turned to see Aurora looking for some opinion in her eyes.

What anyone would least want is a baseball game in full honeymoon.

- If you wish, my love, lets go! - I heard her say. - You have always liked to know stadiums. It must be a historic building for sure.

-Of course it is sir. The Latin American stadium is the home of baseball in Cuba - Eduardo said, but seeing only me. I understood that the guide was keeping his word.

-At the end of the tour you could do us the favor of leaving us at the stadium.

-Of course, sir, but how will you return to the hotel?

-Don't worry, we returned in a taxi.

-Ok, sir, as you order, although I warn you that not many taxis pass by.

-Do not worry. If there is not, we will walk to the hotel. A couple of kilometers are easy, it will help us to know the city.

We arrived at the fifth entrance, drank a glass of rum while appreciating the moon from the stadium and enjoying the excitement of the public.

Best team in the world? Yes, sure. One player came to first with an infield fly. Not even in the league of my city were these deficiencies.

We enjoyed the whole game chatting and screaming on every play. Industriales defeated the representative of Santiago 7 to 6.Eduardo was right. We didn't find a taxi at that time. It was two minutes to midnight. We decided to walk because we knew how to get to the hotel. We passed by the Plaza de la Revolución and took other photos, now with the moon in the background.

Rain was not in our plans, but it was a perfect variant.

Refreshed our tired bodies from walking in the intense island sun. I understood that you can love the rain or hate it and that the difference was her. Beside it, any natural effect was pleasant. We began to dance slowly, right in the middle of the empty square and in half light. It was a giant track made for us, to walk each meter dancing with joy, feeling the rain, the butterflies tickling in the stomach, the humidity and listening to the drops fall as if they were musical notes.

-Imagine a song that you like - Aurora told me. In my mind the chords of the song Amiga, by Miguel Bosé. The lyrics came according to the moment.

-I already did - I replied, sure.

-Now keep dancing and when I tell you, you will sing a phrase you have chosen from that song, which I will also sing mine.

-Hahaha. Okay. I would swear I know what yours is.

-In theory it should be the same. If, according to you, we are ourselves and we always think about the same things. Otherwise you will break my heart. - Her sense of humor was great. She was too smart.

-Hahaha. I don't think it's the same I am disenchanted by Zoé's commercial music.

- Wait, how did you know?

-You are so predictable, Rory.

-And Miguel Bosé, isn't it commercial?

-Hahaha. How did you know?

-Baby, the predictable is you.

-Well, choose your phrase and on the count of three you start singing it. One, two, three.

And each one began to sing the phrase of the song they had chosen.

"There is no one like you who make me feel like this, in a lullaby of stars. I tell you from the soul and with an open heart. You are my eternal love, my guardian angel"

"If I have been what I was, it was because of your body. If I've been night, it was your night who wanted it. If I have been a kiss, it is that my lips learned to be a kiss for you. If I have been what I am, it was in your lap. If I have been life, it was because I gave you life."

I always had brilliant ideas, some crazy, but I loved this one.

We danced like crazy with no rhythm. When we finished, we looked at each other laughing like idiots and we kissed. It was the kindest kiss in the world. So we stayed until the rain stopped and we continued walking along the loving roads of Havana.

It was our last hours of a meteoric honeymoon, but perfect. We went up to pack our bags and went down to the bar, outdoors facing the sea, to drink, she Mojito and I a Bucanero beer. I asked him if he had cigars.

-Are you going to smoke?-I have never smoked a cigar and what better to do with you in the country where they make the most famous cigars in the world.

He recommended a Cohiba number four cigar. I liked its taste. At four in the morning our taxi passed to take us to the airport and fly to Mexico City.

So the last postcard of the honeymoon was my hair tousled by the breeze, surrounding my right arm around her neck, and in my left hand the lit cigar. She with her left hand lifting her Mojito. The waiter captured that image with his mobile phone. Two infinite smiles. We were soulmates.

Chapter 12. My hypothesis of the soul.

Year 2016

It even looked like Déjà vu. Both spiritual guides, both from Catemaco and Benares, predicted the same thing, but in a different language. "You're here to search for her soul," he hammered into my head. That was the same sentence in places so distant from the continent and with totally different cultures. They taught me unknown things.

As a doctor, I always appealed to science and logic, and that was what I planned to do at the time. When I got home, after both trips, I decided to formulate my own hypothesis based on what I had learned from experts in the soul.

The journey along the coast of Veracruz to reach Catemaco and savor some tegogolos on the shore of La Laguna while waiting for an appointment, or being able to touch the sacred waters of the Ganges River with my hands, had been relevant and revitalizing experiences in my life.

My horizons had opened, my conscience. I felt capable of believing things never imagined.

- Shall I find her?

-That nobody can know, only our Supreme Being. You can try it in this life or in the one that follows and only he will decide.

-What should I do?

-Just find the moment, the place, have faith and wait.

I sat down on the bench in the kitchen bar to write in my notebook. I poured myself a tea to relax. If I drank coffee, I wouldn't sleep at night, and I had to rest to be 100 percent physically, if I wanted to find her. I had to develop a strategy to get there. The moment? Only God would know if it is in this life, or the next, or the next, or perhaps never. It all depended on my faith. The place should be a unique and unrepeatable space like our sunsets facing the sea.

"At that precise moment the nuance will be different," I recalled the words of the guides. Sunset should have a different color at that time.

The last factor was faith. My strength to see her was immense, but I had to strengthen them, believe in each abstract belief and take it with fervor. I had to do a ritual to attract that moment with all my strength, so many that her soul approached me.

I remember mentioning Hawking's epitaph. The great man decided to engrave on the tombstone of his grave the formula of entropy of black holes.

"That was probably his guide in finding his soul mate to find him in another life."

Something like a key. So he put it on his tombstone.

- He could have put it anywhere, but putting it on his tombstone was a test of faith, that he would find it.

I had already written down everything necessary to establish this ritual. I felt hallucinating with irrational thoughts, priceless images, original colors. Although for moments I despaired of not knowing so deeply about beliefs, I did not have time for it, I just had to apply them. Do it in faith.

I designed a routine to find her. Every afternoon, when the sun was shining, I decided to go to that place where I would fervently wait until her soul joined me.

Anyone would think it was crazy, but I inexplicably believed in this strategy and thought to follow it to the letter. I dreamed or fantasized about that moment, like a painful one, where my body would melt with heat and my pure essence would remain to merge with her. Joining her was most desirable, although doing it this way was probably a painful feeling. I began to sweat, without stopping, when I imagined my skin turning to dust to fall and stir with the sand, while my soul escaped free to it. Those moments heated me up. I was drinking an ice cold beer by the window to cool off and try to understand that strange feeling of burning veins.

At other times I imagined it as a cold moment, a deadly force freezing my skin, each one of my muscles, veins, arteries, bones, until paralyzing every vital part of my body and freeing my soul, perhaps because death is related to a cold body without the heat of life. On those occasions my room even felt cold. The coolest walls. Although the temperature in my city is always warm, it was an icy feeling like being away in a cabin between heavy snowfalls. She even inspired me to lie down on the sofa, drinking a little coffee, covered by a blanket, while listening to soft music and leaving the windows open so that the wind and breeze blew freely through the house.

Sometimes I believed that I would feel absolutely nothing, that everything would be pleasant, like when our body is anesthetized and feels no pain. I would only see our souls cling together until they become one, take the next unknown step, together. That was the best version because my mind needed to be happy with it again. No suffering from seeing her again.

I thought about every detail, if her essence would come down to me and unite, or I would have to approach her walking among the waves until I slowly lost myself in the depths of the current.

I also imagined the unknown stadium where we would go, what would it be like? Another planet, where we will need a stronger or thinner skin foot. Or an ethereal place where we would be happy, only with our essence. There were millions of possibilities. The important thing was to be together.

The version of meeting her forced me to think about the real environment. Souls do not inhabit the world, not in a tangible way. That left no room for assumptions about my future. So I started by sorting out any unfinished business to imagine our union day as my probable disappearance from the earth. I had to get rid of her pets, a beautiful Pomeranian dog named "Baby", and some stunningly colored fish.

It couldn't be so wicked to leave and drift. So I looked for people with sympathy for these animals. Her friend Mayte was in charge of taking care of "Baby" and I left the fish with her tender little cousin Lili.

That day I invited the neighbor to have a couple of beers to ask him please, if I went away for several days, to come into my house and disconnect everything. I left him a copy of my keys.

Over the weekend I traveled to where my parents lived. I had years of not seeing them and it was too painful to hug my mother and father knowing that it would probably be the last time. They hugged me excitedly. I strongly resisted the shedding of tears.

I closed all my social networks. I called people with whom I was fighting to ask for forgiveness and to declare myself ready to go with her.

The table was served. I was ready, full of illusions, for that trip. The only thing missing was for her to appear.

Chapter 13. The old crazy man

Year 2023

After a week of greeting the crazy old man on the boardwalk, I wondered if I knew more about him. I was intrigued by his words and strange knowledge of my anxieties and search.

I had some theories about him. I thought he was a divine being sent to give me the signal to continue my daily ritual. The second one was a soul and only I could see it. The third was that he was an ordinary person, that he had lost his mind and that everything was the product of his wild imagination due to the consumption of prohibited substances. However, I did not hit on any of my theories.

I finished my routine and approached him offering him a cigarette. I had noticed that he was lifting butts to give them the last pull. I did not smoke, but I also lit one to accompany him and be empathetic with him. I coughed a couple of times.

- Man, put that down. It will kill you - the old man recommended a bit jokingly.

- Right now, what I fear the least is death, sir. - I replied with disdain.

-I know, boy.

-How come you know? Why do you say you know about my pain?

-I've been in the city all my life, boy. I know it right and back. From beginning to end. I know its people and your misfortune with the girl from the Bessi. It was tragic to leave so young.

Apparently he only knew the tragedy, but not the theory of souls.

-Yes, it was very sad, but I hope someday to be with her again - I said about to put out my cigarette and continue on my way.

-You'll be with her soon, son.

His words intrigued me, but this time I did think he was just playing with me.

-Ah yes, and how do you know? You have a magic ball - I asked him, with a little sarcasm.

-It is not necessary to have a magic ball to know the laws of the universe and nature.

-I think so, sir, have a great day - I said goodbye as I handed him the full pack of tobacco. Night was beginning to fall.

-Just have faith, son. The day will come. I can perceive the closeness of her close soul and I don't say it in space, but in time.

-Stop playing with me, sir. Those are fantasies that no one believes.

-I just tell you that the day is near. You also feel it, that's why you come more motivated, excited to see her again.

- Do you believe in these things? - I questioned him.

-Of course. They are divine rules that are in nature - answered the old man now turned into an almost Greek philosopher in my eyes.

-And how is it that you know these divine laws?

- What motivates you to learn? - He answered with another question. Fear or pain? I felt it too many years ago. On May 29, 2000, my daughter Sofía disappeared. You imagine the anguish of her mother and mine. But the fatal blow was when they found her lifeless body on the beach. Can you imagine the pain? I remember the hug she gave me when she left the house and told me "see you in a while dad: I love you".

The old man began to cry. I handed him some paper and we lit another tobacco. Immediately he continued telling me:

-Only two things were going through my mind, seeking revenge or how to hear from her again. Her mother passed away in pain. I was left alone.

-I went to Benares in India to find answers - I said with the intention of stopping the suffering of the man.

-I can imagine it. You can go to the end of the world when you feel that endless pain, but honestly you didn't need to go that far. The answers will always be the same anywhere in the world.

That old man generated confidence in me. Their foul smells no longer bothered me. I even felt like hugging him.

His questions kept giving me light:

-And was it then that you decided that this will be the place where the moment will find her?

-Yes! I have waited for a long time and will be there for the necessary time.

- I have seen you for years, and until now I noticed in you that security and that faith. It is a sign that you are about to achieve it. Don't give up, son - the man stressed to me as he made parting movements.

-And how are you doing with your package? - I asked him.

-Excellent. If my calculations don't fail, you'll probably stop seeing me soon.

- Then you will be leaving before I am.

- I do not know. It is just a guess. I've been coming here longer.

The old man finally walked away. He completely turned his back on me.

The next day he no longer appeared. A week went by and I never saw him again. Far from worrying about his absence, I was pleased to think that this meeting with the venerable lord had been a mirage, a hallucination.

Some people commented that they had found him dead in an uncertain place. I asked God that, if this man existed, he would be with his sweet Sofia and his beloved wife.

Chapter 14. The funeral

Year 2015

All funerals are infinitely sad. That of the person I loved the most was an ordeal. I wanted to stop time and contemplate her inert body forever.

I thought about cremating her and sharing her ashes with her family. But her father was blunt. Her religion forbade that and preferred her daughter in a grave to pray to. I couldn't object. I felt infinite regret. Because of me they had not enjoyed Aurora in their later years.

I could not refuse. The most difficult moments with Aurora's parents came to mind. They really hated me.

- My daughter needs a man, not a clown like you. - my father-in-law once told me.

I think it was the worst humiliation my life received. We had gathered most of her close relatives to break the news of our upcoming marriage bond.

- Sir, I promise to be worthy to belong to your family.- was the first thing I managed to answer.

-I don't want someone like you in my family! Surely you are equal to him, weak, unable to make important decisions, without the guts to achieve your goals.

There seemed to be old quarrels between her family and mine that Rory and I were unaware of. We didn't care in the least. My parents from the beginning of the relationship had moved to another city. They sensed this outcome, but since their love for me was so great that they decided to walk away before it was a problem, but they appeared when I needed them the most.

Pulling the trigger would be a pleasure. Thus, it would end the life of who made fun of my father. I started stroking the trigger with the pad of my index finger, when I heard Rory scream:

-If you do, we can never be together - she sentenced me.

-Come on, don't be a coward Juan Martin. I already told you that as long as I live, Aurora will never leave this house. Show a little courage, do it.

I was terrified just thinking about not being with her. Her pleas sounded like orders. I threw the gun as far as possible.

Her father was imposing, large, robust, with short fuse. I don't know how I had the courage to take her hand and get out of there, at a fast pace, almost running.

And yet, after 15 years of nurturing hatred and rancor in our hearts, seeing each other again was disconcerting.

My father-in-law approached. I expected the worst, but held me tight. He was crying like a child, holding me. I also couldn't contain the crying. We had both lost the love of our lives.

We said nothing to each other, no complaints, no words of encouragement. We act as if we don't have a warlike past, like the family we never were, after so many wasted years. It was just a hug that spoke for us and cured us.

At times I wished that the clock did not keep ticking and that the first rays of the sun did not arrive. We were all at mass. My mother hugged me and tried to comfort me like when I was a child and told me that everything would be fine. Its scent reassured me. My father, a man of few words, hugged me tight. Without them I would not have survived the funeral.

When my mother asked me if I had eaten anything, it was when I realized that I had not eaten for 24 hours. Nothing fancied me, not an espresso, not a buccaneer beer, not a mojito.

I dragged my chair closest to the coffin. They had scented it. I could perceive it among the dozens of crowns. When the funeral services entered the room I felt a blow to my soul. It was time for farewell. I watched everything in slow motion, as they carried away the coffin, people floating and voices drowning.

I let her parents go in the float. I went in my parents' van.

Everyone encouraged me, but I was in limbo.

While the funeral procession was taking place around the boardwalk, the sun fell on the sea that looked better than ever. It was the same route, holding hands, that I did with Aurora. I cried harder on the way to the pantheon.

Until we finally reached the fork where the road ended by the sea.

A kilometer from her final home, I burst into tears. I remembered when Aurora told me that she had never seen her father cry. I think he never did because he had never felt pain like today.

Why do we waste 15 years as a big family? Perhaps a better relationship would have helped Aurora's health. So many doubts and questions assailed me. I was very confused.

The tapping of each spoon gathering the concrete mixture to repel its grave were already the last "tick tock" of the time we had left. Her father spoke a few words and thanked me for making her happy. I never expected that, and although I didn't return to Aurora, it was a consolation. I was the first to throw sand into her coffin, then I threw a cut rose from the garden of our house and finally I threw a sheet of paper, where I wrote all my rest. I listened to the prayers to the beat of those present and then a downpour silence came, as if announcing the end of the world, of my universe. It had dawned hot, but in the last strokes the sky was heartbroken.

They all ran. We only resist the family. Minutes later, my parents and in-laws crossed themselves and left the place. I was alone with her. I always loved her exclusively. There it was.

-See you soon, JuanMa - I managed to hear in my transformed pain, with rain and tears, in a hallucination.

Final Chapter

Februay 23 of 2023

There are such perfect days. Everything prostrates before you. You can smell the flowers from the neighboring garden. The sky shines unrepentantly and you can barely look at it. It bothers your eyes, but it still doesn't stop being nice.

You listen to the crowing of the first roosters announcing the new day. You enjoy the aroma of coffee and its flavor feels more intense. From the first sip it manages to stimulate your metabolism. Now I feel different, as if powered by a high voltage discharge. I go out into the street to carry out my routine. Sometimes my body felt tired from working all day. I thought about resting 24 hours, missing the ritual, but it stops me from thinking that today could be the day. Although I felt my head explode from the stress of work, I returned to walk the same path every evening.

It is rare to feel active in the afternoon. Normally stress begins to take its toll on me, stemming from the physical and emotional wear and tear of a daily struggle to improve the health of my patients. However, that day I did not leave pending tasks in the office.

From the fridge I took a bottle of Balvenie whiskey, 25, a flashy gift from my friend Rafael on my last birthday. I was a fan of that drink for its vanilla flavor. I saved it for a special moment. The last time I had taken Balveni was when I married Rory. Now I take the bottle of Whiskey and put it in my backpack. I also pull a bottle of water and another of gatorade. I took the photo of our honeymoon and put it in the back pocket of my shorts that day. Then, from one of the closet drawers, I took out a purple T-shirt as a gift from Rory, with which we debuted as a couple in our first race together.

Those five kilometers were different from any other competition. Her company made the difference, and although I could barely pronounce a word because my physical condition was not as strong as hers, it was a pleasure to answer every question she asked me.

Being with her gave me the strength to resist the jog and coordinate my brain to answer correctly. I kept that shirt from that day because it became special, I could not wear it more times because it would wear out and probably even fade, and it would be another item of clothing in some bazaar or in the garbage. Reading the front of the shirt made me bend a little and shed a tear on the cedar wood that had given it an old-fashioned smell. "I love you Grumpy", it was read and on the reverse side only the initial of her first name and mine.

At that time I was using a device to measure kilometers and calories, which I had received as a gift on my last birthday. She had never used it, but fortunately now it turned on.

I took a shower and shaved to keep my date flawless. I even put on gel. I opened the door behind the bathroom mirror and there it was, keeping the damn lotion that made me use it the whole time we were together. It was the last bottle left, not only in my house, probably on Earth. They had discontinued it. I found out online that it was still being sold in Panama. I poured a little over my face, chest, back, neck and legs. Smelling that aroma caused me a mixture of pain, rancor, but also nostalgia to relive every moment with her. I felt devastated and dropped crying among the wood of the drawers, isolated, where no one could see me. I turned on the music player and there was no better song at the time. That old group that we sometimes heard together at a concert.

Who do you need? Who do you love? When you come undone
Hey child stay wilder than the wind and blow me in to cry.

What better time to wear old sneakers, the ones we buy in the same style and color. We never released them together. She ran a half-marathon that for work reasons I could not accompany her, and I premiered mine for breaks in a medical congress.

Rain was forecast. The day looked beautiful, with no apparent trace of rain. Anyway, I took precautions and kept a small umbrella in my backpack.

I disconnected electrical appliances from the house. In a kitchen notebook, which I used as a blog, I wrote a small message to feel confident. Cannot be! At that moment I felt like a toast with butter and jam. I made it for myself in record time and also put it in my backpack.

I did not lock the house. Who could go in there? There was nothing of value. Everything was material. The only valuable thing was her and me.

I looked at the sky. Dark clouds seemed to be visible. Today the weather forecast was so accurate, it was scary. I put on my head a cap from the San Francisco 49ers, the team we always want to see live in Santa Clara. We never could.

Always the damn time and the occupations.

I started jogging towards the boardwalk. I quickly recovered the state of mind I had when I first got home. I felt every step a meter less to reach my goal. That was my mindset when I didn't want to go running. This was how apathy overcame. Instead of thinking negatively, I assumed that each step was one meter less. Each day was 24 hours less for the desired moment. I was absorbed, without turning around to avoid distractions and listening to music with my headphones.

I felt I could run 10 kilometers. My chest was inflated, strong. My legs were not complaining. The blocks that separated my house from the sea passed by my sight in a jiffy. I was running faster than ever. I inhaled deeply through my nose and released all the air screaming like a madman, expelling toxins, any sin committed the night before.

The sea was still visible a kilometer away. How lucky we are the natives of the coast. There is no more pleasant, relaxing, mesmerizing, intoxicating feeling than being close to the wild noise of the ocean waves.

This day I ran through all the sand that surrounds that stretch. While jogging along the way, I got rid of my tennis shoes and put them in my backpack. I wanted to feel the freshness of the sea water brushing the soles of my feet. Suddenly there was an unusual effect. The sky clouded over, but it did not rain. A rainbow slowly began to form. I kept running like a runaway animal. Repeating to myself that it was already the day. I was getting faster and faster. The sky was like an eclipse in the North, dark cloudy in the South and with a radiant sun over the sea.

The images were common, although the scene was unique.

It was observed greyish in all its shades until almost reaching black from West to East, limiting with a light blue from the most intense burned by the rays of the sun to the clearest flooded with white clouds, from East to West.

In every meter traveled in that landscape, that strange rainbow began to form. They were not the usual seven colors, but a combination of antagonistic nuances in the sky. I kept running faster and faster, and so I felt lighter. The cool water touching my feet with the last breath of the waves, filled me with immense energy, like a drug stimulating my senses. I felt myself floating on the soft waves, like a thin leaf flying aimlessly. My legs, feet and hands were no longer moving voluntarily, but were directed by someone else.

However, with what little strength I had left, I kept running, desperate, on the sand and the water of the sea, like a marathon runner a few meters from reaching the finish line. I felt that feeling, although to a lesser extent when I was exhausted when I saw the end of the five-kilometer race.

My body felt a rush of energy and automatically started to run stronger. I felt the legs without pain, an imposing force.

The closer I saw the goal, my legs ran faster. I was flying in those moments. I could hear Rory in the bravery of the crash of the waves, the closer I got to that nuanced effect in the sky, the more salty than the sea I could feel her taste.

A moment later I began to run, no longer from East to West, but from South to North, heading towards the depth of the ocean, towards the horizon. I tried to turn to shore, but my neck was stiff. My brain couldn't give the order to flip. It was as if my mind was programmed to just look straight ahead, which was becoming more and more beautiful.

The image evoking the water and the oil was changing as I got closer to that landscape. It was a slow approach, but every inch forward the fusion of those nuances was causing those different nuances sought for years. That motivated me even more to continue running without rest, although the water was already beginning to reach my chest and wet my backpack, which must have felt heavier, but it was not. I didn't feel anything, but I still got rid of it. I left it floating. I did not care.

In theory, each step should sink me into the salty and hot waters, however, from the moment the waves hit my chest I stopped submerging. It seemed strange to me to be almost a kilometer away, and the water could not cover me completely. There was probably a long flat part in the sand, although it sounded illogical.

As when meditating, now my body felt relaxed, light, as if floating on the sea. I stopped feeling the rubbing of the sand on my feet, although I continued running and propelling myself out to sea. Maybe the fatigue made me lose my sensibility on my feet.

As I got closer to the rainbow, I had the sensation that it was moving towards me. It would not be long in coming. I felt that my legs were like propellers of a huge ship spinning at high speed because they continued to run, but they were no longer touching the bottom.

On any other occasion this would have seemed out of reality, but in those moments I felt everything was possible. I was about, according to my hope, to achieve the miracle never imagined, to see her again. Anything else that seemed implausible would go unnoticed, like the fact that I wasn't diving.

It was totally incomprehensible, but possible up to a point. So many boats stranded on the coast of my city had created wells and slopes causing accidents frequently.

It was no longer understandable as the water level dropped to my heels. I could see as if my legs were wings flying fast, moving towards the horizon. The feeling is indescribable, sometimes we have dreamed that we fly.

Flying is the greatest pleasure. At that moment I found myself defying gravity and reality. My brain kept dictating the same instructions to move forward and although it was in a different way my body continued towards the horizon that was getting closer. My walking tour could not be compared to the hundreds of kilometers that I floated on the waves.

I knew it, it was not a product of my imagination. The nuances of the horizon seemed to indicate the way to it. It seemed like a dream, a fallacy, a wish, but at that moment it was the most beautiful reality.

I will not describe the sensations, emotions, feelings, colors and characteristics that I observed and experienced before reaching the horizon of unique nuances. I will do it for two reasons, the least important because I had no words to describe what I could feel or live there. It was like being in another world, on another planet, maybe it was what you thought of heaven.

The second and most important reason is because when entering there I could see the most sublime image, and waited for so long. I tried to cry from the emotion, but no tears came out. My heart felt comforted. I had very little hair. I had lost itbecause of the stress of not having her by my side. I got some wrinkles accumulated by the sleeplessness and pain of her departure. My body was more robust.

I felt sorry because she looked perfect. Her huge green eyes accompanied by the nuances of the horizon looked light lilac and shone like a diamond. Her cheeks did not have a single blemish, her body was covered in a white trail that radiated white light. I was thinking of saying a thousand things to her, but at that moment my body pounced on her. I wanted a hug from her. I was like that for several minutes, with the sensation of crying without tears, until my body began to fuse with hers.

Everything went so fast. I just felt happiness. At that time I understood all the definitions of soul, that of when we had no form, when we were an intangible entity and the same essence. I understood little, but I just let myself go, confident that she would have an answer to everything. We no longer existed. We were an essence and still remained the perfect couple.

-I thought we would never see each other again - I heard her voice, sublime, in total frenzy.

- "You have no idea what I went through to get here! - I replied. - I thought it was crazy. Only faith kept me standing looking for you on the horizon. Believing those theories and holding on knowing that it was likely could never happen was complicated. I know. Imagine, if it was difficult for me to get here, for you it must have been an ordeal.
- It was, but no ordeal will ever separate me from you.

- Now I know. Did you know that only one soul in a million achieves what we achieve today?

-I don't care about the odds. I knew I would be with you again.

-My only concern is your family that you left on Earth.

-Do not think about mundane and material things at this time. For the world I left a note in the kitchen of our house.

"I will not come back. I ran away towards happiness"

The clock said 6:27 p.m.

THE END